A Question of Import

Detective Twyle, Volume 1

Rachel Caren Kisala

Published by Rachel Caren Kisala, 2023.

A QUESTION OF IMPORT

First edition. March 15, 2023.

ISBN: 979-8215946374

Written by Rachel Caren Kisala.

For John Arthur Kisala,

who convinced me that you don't have to wait until you're
grown up to start writing stories.

Prologue

TO GOVERNOR AZIEL THORNE, salutations.

We of the Law Enforcement Reform Oversight Commission have reviewed your proposal and are most heartily in favor of your choice of Lieutenant Everett Twyle as leader of an experimental team to explore and promote a new culture of police work. His record and professional reputation are above reproach; he has never been known to take a bribe of any size, all formal complaints against him have been thoroughly investigated both by the existing structures of the police and by this Commission and have been found to be without merit, and his superiors describe him as a man who thinks things through before he acts. I am not sure they meant this as praise, but for our purposes it may as well be.

As for his personal life, if he has made any grave errors, they have been made with such discretion as to stand up to our scrutiny of his moral fiber. There are suggestions and guesswork as to his inclinations, but knowing Your Grace as I do, I do not believe that this is anything you will find objectionable, even should it prove true.

The Commission does wish to raise for further discussion the issue of who else will be on this team. We are all agreed to giving Twyle and his men such a broad mandate as to be answerable to almost no one, but such power should not be given lightly. In short, madam, are you insistent that Twyle be allowed full and free choice over the composition of his team? We would prefer that each member should be vetted and approved by the Commission to the same extent that Twyle himself has been, or at least that we should approve a list of candidates from whom he could choose. As the orders are written now, there is not even a requirement that he choose men who are already members of the police force! We will bow to your wisdom in this, but it is the advice of this Commission that at least some forethought and restriction ought to be placed on this.

Yours sincerely,
The Law Enforcement Reform Oversight Commission
Glenward Louzain, Chairman

Chapter 1

THE RIVER WINDS ITS way through the city like a drunk trying to find the shortest path to his bed. From the right perspective - perhaps the eyes of a goose, circling overhead looking for a place to rest on its flight south - it sparkles, a faint purplish-grey sheen almost entirely hidden by the gleam of morning sunlight. Only in one particularly stumble-footed twist where the river nearly doubles back on itself do other colors show through the glare - vivid pinks, reds, greens, colors that never belonged in the same patch of water. The bend is bounded by a dam at each end and, between them, the water leaps and bubbles - and occasionally sizzles. One goose, unfortunate enough to try drinking directly from the river's foam, lets out an indignant squawk and a flurry of sparks that very briefly sets the damp deadfall on the bank smoking.

The lowlands south of the river, known locally as the Mire, has never been built up as much as other neighborhoods. Too urban to be called a swamp, too soggy to be called anything else, a few factories have been thrifty enough to snap up bits of cheap land and erect flimsy structures, but even slumlords wouldn't dream of trying to put apartments on the soft ground.

People call it home anyway, of course. There are always people desperate enough to sleep wherever they won't be chased off. But no one builds walls and roofs for them.

As the ground rises, sturdier constructions take over - schools, shops, temples, and, far enough away that the backyard won't give way to open fens, the homes of those whose lifestyle includes certainty about where they'll sleep tonight, with clear boundaries defined by fences and hedges. Crisply painted houses and perfectly coiffed gardens suggest that here, at least, the city was shaped by the hand of man and not by natural geography. About a third of the lawns are currently occupied by a woman trimming grass and shrubbery, all of them somehow managing the sharp and unwieldy tools without slicing their wide skirts and aprons.

A particularly keen observer might note that one or two hedge-clippers open and close on empty air over a spot that's already perfectly smooth. No one has started to speculate out loud - yet - but a pair of brown-uniformed men lounging on the front steps of one house are drawing the quiet attention of the neighbors, pulling their eyes away from pruning.

Oblivious to the keen ears of the neighborhood women, the two men are making brusque conversation.

"Nah, the dam's getting worked up over nothing. Girl will waltz back in time for dinner and we'll both get pats on the back from the brass. Easiest day's work we've ever done."

"I don't know, Al." The second uniformed man adjusts his badge self-consciously, staring at a slightly darker patch on his partner's shirt. Grease from the takeout they ate together three days ago. Haig Lulling himself will never be the neatest dresser in the world and probably doesn't have a leg to stand on criticizing anyone else, but that's never stopped him from doing it. "The father took the day off work, would he have done that if everything was fine? He says the little missy's never run off before, and I think I believe him. And I told you yesterday, that shirt's got a date with the laundry. Should've worn your spare."

"Spare's even dirtier." Al Kambyr rolls his eyes. "And yeah, okay, first time for everything, the parents are all worried because dolly's never done this before. I still say she walked off on her own, and she'll come back when she's tired or hungry. Girls get flighty at that age, the womb starts wandering right up to the head and makes them do all sorts of crazy things. This one girl I used to know, she..."

Lulling points at his partner's shirt, grateful for the interruption - Kambyr's tall tales can go on for hours. "Your pocket's shaking."

"Yeah, yeah." Kambyr pulls a tin square out of his pocket; a queasy-looking grey-green swirl on the surface makes it hard to see the raised pattern pressed into the metal. It stops vibrating at his touch, and he lifts it to a few inches from his ear. "Kambyr."

"Dispatch. You're still on scene at 421 Larch Street?"

"Yeah."

"I have new orders for you and Lulling: hold in place and prepare to turn your case over to Captain Twyle."

"I've got you on a bad connection, dispatch, could lose you any minute. Can you repeat?"

"Your orders are to hold..."

Kambyr drops the audiocast back into his pocket, cutting the connection, and grunts. "Like we need that fancy-assed team taking this over. I tell ya, we have it solved already."

"Mhmm." Lulling doesn't give voice to the question of why Kambyr bothered to hang up on the dispatcher. Twyle and his handpicked detectives tend to get what they want; if they've decided this case needs to be looked over and brought up to reform standards, well, no amount of shoving fingers in ears will make them go away.

A gentle chime from inside the house announces a call coming in on the built-in audiocast - larger and more reliable than the little cards the cops carry. Lulling smiles a little "I told you so" smile, even though he hadn't told anyone anything, and makes sure he's the farther of the two from the door when the missing doll's mother appears to let them know there's a call for them inside. Let Kambyr take this call, too.

Officer Lulling's attention is still on the door after his partner has gone inside, his smug smile betraying his sense of misplaced superiority, and he doesn't notice the man in the crisp suit strolling down the street.

He's probably the only one. Most of the women settle for corner-of-the-eye glances, but a few - widows, perhaps, or women with old-maid sisters who've so far refused to be trapped into marriage - are bold enough to look at him directly, noting the confident walk, the trim waistline and squared-off shoulders, the dark hair going to a distinguished salt-and-pepper just over the ears. The sound of hedge-trimmers fades almost entirely as he passes, only the determined shwip-shwip-shwip of the most serious pruners remaining.

The newcomer comes to a stop behind the still-oblivious policeman. "Report, constable."

Lulling spins around, faster than he probably meant to. "Captain Twyle, sir! Sorry, I didn't...hear you..." He gathers his composure. "Missing girl, sir. She'll be back any minute now. This really isn't worth your time, sir."

"I didn't ask if it was worth my time, I asked for a report on the case."

Standing at attention, Lulling's shoulders twitch but he stops himself before it turns into a shrug. "Seventeen-year-old Brienda Woolsyth was discovered missing by her parents this morning. Her father called the police, who dispatched us from our usual patrol in this vicinity. He stayed home from work, which is a mercy because you can never get sense out of the mother in these situations."

"It's a wonder how much more sense people make when you actually listen." Twyle's harsh tone is entirely unnoticed by the constable. "What else have you learned?"

This time Lulling does go so far as to shrug. "That's it, sir. That's the entire case. There's nothing more to it."

"There's always more to it." Twyle locks eyes with the constable, the thought "I wonder if it's worth the time it'd take to tell you off right now" clear on his face. Lulling's lack of reaction to the stare suggests it probably isn't. "Take your partner and go back to your usual patrol. I want written reports from both of you on my desk by the end of the day, but you're to have no further interaction with this case."

A QUESTION OF IMPORT

The Captain passes but doesn't acknowledge Constable Kambyr on his way into the house. His attention is all on the distraught parents, in the kitchen at the back of the house, talking quietly to...someone. The man is tall, young, and wears his blond hair artfully rumpled and his shirt with the top button undone, though it is impeccably clean. A police badge dangles from the pocket of his dark blue vest almost like an afterthought.

"Morris," Twyle acknowledges - and, though Mr. and Mrs. Woolsyth aren't in a state to notice, anyone else would surely hear the note of displeasure in his voice.

"Your man moves fast, Captain," Mr. Woolsyth says, standing and offering Twyle his hand. "He got here just before you did. Came in the back door as that constable was leaving. Ought to be commended."

"Yes, I'll speak to him about that later." Twyle aims a glare over Mrs. Woolsyth's head at Ayden Morris, who is lounging comfortably against the counter. "Has he already gotten the details of your daughter's disappearance from you?"

"Oh, yes, he's been very thorough," Mrs. Woolsyth says, talking fast and blinking too much in that way some people do when they're trying to distract themselves from crying. "Much more than those other two...well, I wouldn't want to speak ill of them but they seemed a bit..."

"Dim as a ha'penny lamp, the pair of them," her husband says, clearly not sharing her restraint.

"My team and I will have more questions for you later, but for now, I need to look at her room, and I need you to do something for me while I do that." The Woolsyths both look at him expectantly. "I need two lists: one of any friends or family members Brienda might trust enough to turn to if she's in trouble and needs help, the other of everyone she's interacted with in the last few weeks. Even store clerks, delivery boys, cab drivers - everyone. Include as much information as you can, full names, addresses, workplaces."

"Of course," Mr. Woolsyth says. His wife is already reaching for a notepad and pen from the table in front of the massive wall-mounted audiocast. The large crystal at the center of the metal-and-glass framework still glows faintly, especially where Kambyr touched it - his palm-print shines a vivid red against the fainter pinkish-orange of the rest of the crystal sphere. "Her room is upstairs, all the way to the back, on the right." At a sharp look from his wife, he adds, "I can show you up, of course."

Twyle shakes his head and waves the man to sit down. He starts to leave the room, then looks back at Morris, who isn't following. Twyle's face tightens slightly, the visual equivalent of a sigh. Morris tosses off a lazy salute, pushes himself away from the counter, and joins Twyle.

It isn't a very remarkable room. The bed hasn't been made, the sheets are rumpled enough that it's clearly been slept in at some point - though whether that point was last night, well. The laundry isn't put away either; several days' worth of shirts and underthings are piled on the floor in the general vicinity of an empty hamper. The pale blue ruffled bedspread has slid to the carpet, covering the edge of another pile of clothes; the matching bedskirt has been lifted at one side, no doubt for easier access to the shoes shoved under the bed.

There are several pens by the lamp on the nightstand, but no sign of paper or, more to Twyle's interest, journals.

A quick search of the classic hiding places reveals a misplaced sock under the mattress, an assortment of underwear in the underwear drawer, and an interesting collection of hair and dust bunnies in the back of the closet.

There really isn't anything to see here. Just an ordinary second floor bedroom at the back of the house, with a single window looking out over the neighbor's yard. Twyle checks it, but it's securely latched from the inside.

"Should get the wonder boy in here to do a tracking spell."

Twyle raises an eyebrow at Morris. "From her bedroom? It wouldn't know where to point because everywhere she ever went, she went from here. Hold that for when we know where she went after bedtime last night."

Chapter 2

THE CLEANERS HAVE REARRANGED the furniture again; one chair's been placed behind Twyle's massive desk, two opposite facing it, and a fourth positioned discreetly in a corner at a petite writing desk. Someone has put a small bunch of flowers alongside the inkwell and fresh paper.

Veryn Alsace leaves that chair where it is and takes one of the two in front of her boss's desk. She doesn't fidget with her hair or re-check her makeup, showing an uncommon poise for a woman shy of twenty. Waiting for Twyle to arrive and start the meeting, she has nothing to do but stare at the painting behind his desk, hung where everyone who walks into the office will see it - or, more cynically, where he'll have his back to it and never have to look at it. Alsace has tried not looking herself, but the subject's very large, very pink face keeps pulling her eyes back to it. Anyway, looking at it keeps her back to the delicate secretary's station.

"Morning." Morris - technically Detective Morris, if he were the kind of man to whom that sort of title would stick - slides into the seat next to her, glances to see what she's looking at, and smiles. "Why does he keep that godawful painting, anyway?"

"Because it was a gift from Governor Thorne," Twyle says from the doorway. Neither of the two inside seems startled. "Painted by her mother and given to me on my latest promotion, I suspect because she couldn't find anyone to give her money for it." His head turns, taking in the full room. "Where's Sedwin?"

"Here! I'm here. Sorry, sir." Running into the office behind Twyle, notebook clutched in one arm, Derri Sedwin looks on the verge of tripping. He dresses more practically than some wizards, favoring loose grey pants instead of robes, and he manages to get his feet under him as he slows. It takes him a few moments of looking around the room to spot the last chair in its corner; he lifts it awkwardly, narrowly avoiding knocking the flowers off the secretary's desk, and moves it closer to the other chairs. As he settles into the seat he almost meets Alsace's eyes, but looks away quickly.

No one suggests that she should have taken the secretary's seat.

It doesn't take Twyle long to outline Brienda Woolsyth's situation. "The parents don't believe she ran away, and neither do I," he concludes, "but I do feel that we ought to seriously discuss the possibility."

Sedwin pages through his notebook. "Statistically, a girl that age, from that neighborhood or one like it...if she'd left of her own will, she'd either be back before she was missed, or would have turned up at a friend's house by now."

"She's seventeen," Alsace comments. "One has to wonder if it even counts as running away at that age. If she dragged a young man and a magistrate along with her, the law would treat her as a married adult. Why does being single lose her the right to make her own decisions? If we find her and it does turn out she doesn't want to go home, I say we wish her well and send her on her way."

"If," Twyle says. Alsace meets his eyes for nearly twenty seconds before she looks away. Morris smirks; Sedwin's eyes dart back and forth between Alsace and the boss. "Our job is to find her, not to decide who's got the right to tell her what to do. Do you think she ran away?" One eyebrow raised, Twyle continues to look at Alsace. Sedwin twitches nervously, but Morris just sits, patient and still.

There's silence while the young woman thinks about it. "I think - barring some well-hidden secret - she had no reason to. No one's mentioned anything recent and specific that could have precipitated a decision like this. No fight with her parents - beyond what's normal for any young woman. No trouble at her school, no boyfriend, no problems with her friends. I think Sedwin is right, even if she fought with her parents and left the house, she'd have run straight to a friend. She has plenty of those, by all accounts. I think she was abducted."

"By whom?" Twyle's eyes finally move, opening the question to the room.

"Someone she knew," Morris says, his quiet voice full of absolute certainty. "A girl that age is hard to control, you can't just give her a sweet and tell her to behave. You want to keep her quiet and contained, you'll have to drug her or chain and gag her. That's a lot of work, and not worth the bother unless you're absolutely certain you'll have plenty of time alone with her and no one coming after you - or unless you want that specific girl. Her parents called us before breakfast, whoever took her wasn't willing to settle for a girl who wouldn't be missed."

No one disagrees. The sound of Sedwin's pen dropping to the floor breaks the moment. As he bends to pick it up, Twyle nods, once. He takes the two folded lists of names the girl's parents gave him out of his pocket and puts them on his desk.

"We start with the most-trusted list. Tell them it's because we're hoping one of them may have heard from her, but you know what you're looking for."

"We do?" Sedwin fidgets with his pen, nearly drops it again, sets it firmly down on top of his notebook, and leaves it alone.

Alsace rolls her eyes. "Signs of obsession or an unusual amount of interest in Brienda, evidence of abusive actions or attitudes towards Brienda or other family members, secretive behavior, deviations from routine over the last few days."

"Right, right." Sedwin flips through his notebook, dislodging the pen again. "I've got that here somewhere."

"Try putting it up here," Twyle says, tapping his own forehead. His smile softens the words into a piece of advice rather than a rebuke.

"Yes, sir, I'll try."

"We'll interview in pairs for now. Sedwin, with me." The wizard looks relieved. "Alsace, start with the mother, she might say things to a woman that she wouldn't tell me. Take Morris with you, and both of you try to be nice to these people until we know more."

Chapter 3

THERE'S A WINDOW, BUT when Brienda finally hauls her head high enough to look out it - they woke her by throwing a bucketful of water through the bars on the door, and her hands are still damp from trying to get it out of her eyes - she can't see much. The wall of another building, close enough to block the view, far enough away that she couldn't possibly jump across to it, even if she could squeeze through the high, narrow opening. The muddy ground, far below. It could be any alley in Dreeve.

It could be any alley in any city.

She thinks not. She hopes not. She was grabbed from behind and wrestled unceremoniously into the back of a wagon and, while she wasn't able to see where it took her, she's fairly certain she was conscious the whole time and the ride wasn't that long.

With a heavy sigh, she drops down from the window and tries to make herself comfortable sitting on the bare tile floor, back against the wall, eyes on the door.

She's almost fallen asleep again when something hits her in the shoulder. "Time to get some food in you, if you're done sleeping it off."

The hall outside the door is dim enough that she can't see much, just a bulky, man-shaped shadow, but the voice is the same as the one that had laughed when she was drenched awake. Not wanting to give him a reason to laugh again - to do something to her that would make him laugh - she fumbles in the shadows on the floor next to her until she finds the lump of hard bread he'd thrown at her.

Sleeping what off? she wonders. She doesn't think they'd drugged her. Maybe they've mistaken her for someone else, someone who might have been out on a binge last night?

"Eat up, dolly. Sooner you're steady on your feet, the better this'll be."

Better for whom, he doesn't say. She nibbles cautiously at the edges of the bread.

Chapter 4

"SHE'S A GOOD GIRL, you know." Stanzy Woolsyth spoons sugar into her tea and starts stirring, either not remembering or not caring that she already sweetened it. "I mean, she drives me absolutely out of my head sometimes, but it's the age, you know? I hated my mother when I was seventeen, and now every time I fight with Brienda I remember that and send my mum flowers to thank her for not killing me."

"Mm." Detective Alsace stirs her own tea slowly, voicing a wordless "I'm listening, keep going" kind of sound.

"She's never done anything like this. When I clear my head enough to think about how she's acting the worst I can really say about her is she keeps her room a bit of a mess. I hate to let people see it like this but the men said not to move anything in there in case it might mean something."

"What do you think when your head isn't clear?" Alsace asks, casually and neutrally, no judgment implied.

Stanzy freezes for a moment, spoon stopping in mid-stir, face waiting for the next expression. Her hand retraces the path to the sugar-bowl and adds a spoon to her tea before her face moves again. "Oh, I get mad at her for not listening when she's asked to do something, for chatting with her friends and slacking off on her homework, for sleeping too late, I think I've called her lazy to her face a time or two. I wish I hadn't because she really is a good girl and now I'm afraid she doesn't know that."

Alsace nods sympathetically, her chestnut-brown bun bobbing up and down with the motion. "When was your most recent fight, and what set it off?"

"Day before yesterday," Stanzy says, tipping another spoon of sugar into her tea. "She'd planned ahead of time to go to a friend's after school, but she knows to be home for dinner. That's always the rule. She wasn't, so when Prewitt got home from work I sent him around to bring her back. She was absolutely livid, I could hear them shouting at each other from halfway down the block. All the neighbors must have heard. I stepped in as soon as she got through the door so he could have his dinner while it was hot. It wasn't the worst fight we've ever had, she knew she'd stayed out too late, I gave her the lecture and she calmed down and we had a civil meal before it was completely cold."

"Mm." Alsace sips her tea, eyes fixed on the spoon Stanzy is stirring hers with. Will it be one more spoon of sugar or two before it starts overflowing? "What's the name of the friend?"

"Ode Cadalan. They know each other from school, they're the same age. Ode lives just two streets over, I'll get you the address."

"I think I have it already, it was on the list you gave Captain Twyle."

"Oh, both lists, I'm sure. She trusts Ode with everything, and they see each other just about every day." Stanzy starts to reach for the sugar-spoon, pauses, glances at her tea, and continues the motion. Alsace excuses herself before the woman starts stirring again.

The route to Ode's house is a short enough walk that they certainly could have gone back and forth several times a day. Alsace is nearly there by the time Morris, who she left interviewing the husband, catches up with her.

"Let me guess, the father said he had a fight with her two days ago because she stayed too late at a friend's?"

Morris nods. "Parents could've practiced their story together."

"Could've, but I don't think so. I get the impression it was the kind of fight we can get the neighbors to verify."

They find Mrs. Cadalan trimming her lawn, just like half the women on the block. When Alsace asks about Ode, the woman points inside.

The door isn't standing open, but they take that as an invitation. A girl about Brienda's age is slouched in an out-of-place chair in the hall, staring at the wall-mounted crystal audiocast; she perks up immediately when they walk in. "Did you find her?"

"No, not yet," Alsace says. "Are you expecting her to call?"

"Hoping, really, not expecting."

Both detectives nod. "Can we talk in the kitchen?" Alsace asks. "It'll still be close enough to answer if it rings."

Ode nods, picks up her chair, and carries it into the kitchen, where it matches the rest of the breakfast set.

"We have some questions about Brienda," Alsace says, her face fixed in a friendly-yet-bland smile. "We need to know more about what was going on in her life, and we've heard you know her pretty well. How were her relationships? With her parents, with other friends - was there a boyfriend?"

"No, no boyfriend." Ode giggles nervously. "She had crushes, obviously, we both did, but nothing real. And everything else was fine. People like her at school, she gets along great with her parents and teachers."

"She fight with anyone recently?"

Ode shakes her head. "She got along with everyone, really."

Over Ode's head, Alsace and Morris exchange a look.

"I think that'll be all for now," Morris says, "but I'm sure we'll be back a few more times. If she does call, please let us know."

The walk back is just as fast; without much discussion, when they're nearly back to Brienda's house, the two detectives split apart and each target a different one of the omnipresent hedge-clipper-wielding housewives. Morris crosses the street while Alsace ambles over to the house next to Brienda's.

The woman makes no pretense of keeping her attention on her hedge; by the time Alsace gets there she's already set the clippers down. "You're with the police, aren't you? About the Woolsyths' girl?"

Alsace nods. "We're trying to make sure we have all our facts in the right order," she says. "Can you tell me, did Brienda fight with her parents a few days ago?"

"Oh, good heavens, yes. It was three - no, two days ago, it was the day we had the roast for dinner, it was pork and rice the day before. I could hear Stanzy and the girl both shouting fit to wake the dead for twenty minutes straight, but I think they made up in the end. There was some fuss with her father earlier, I think he'd dragged her home from somewhere."

The detective nods thoughtfully again, and jots down a few notes.

"I'll tell you, though, last night - it must have been close to midnight, I'm never up that late but I had a headache and couldn't sleep, thought the air in the garden would help - what do I see but that girl climbing out her bedroom window! I never! I meant to tell Stanzy about it first thing this morning, but then there's been all this fuss and police all over the place."

"Really." About to put her notebook away, Alsace opens it up again. "Did you see anything else?

Chapter 5

"THE WINDOW."

Feet firmly planted on the crisp-cut grass, leaning back to look up at such a precise angle that he misses snagging his jacket on the hedge by about a quarter inch, Morris stares at Brienda's bedroom window. Alsace, standing a more comfortable distance from the bushes, matches his pose. "Mm-hmm."

"This window." Morris shifts a few inches to the left, to look at a different angle.

"That's what the neighbor said."

"This window which was locked from inside."

"Yup."

"You think the parents locked it after she left?" Morris asks.

"Stranger things have happened." Alsace takes a step closer to the house and looks up at a steeper angle, examining the window from almost directly below it.

"Where's our expert on the strange, anyway? We need a tracking spell."

"Boss didn't give me an ETA, he just said soon. I think they wanted to wrap up some interviews at her school first."

"Great." Morris paces over to the house, grasps the jutting wood trim, and pulls himself up by one hand, experimentally. "Could you climb this?"

"Probably."

He drops back to the ground. "I'd be surprised if the parents locked the window, they seemed on the level. So did the neighbor. But you know..."

"Ode was lying to us. Yeah."

"What about, do you think?"

Alsace shrugs. "Could be anything from cutting class to running an international drug-smuggling ring. Probably not a suicide pact, I didn't get that sense from Ode, but that's about the only thing I can rule out."

"You think Ode killed her?" Morris's tone is light and speculative, but that doesn't make the question any less weighty. Alsace has to think about it.

"If she had, I don't think she'd have neglected to tell us about that fight Brienda had with her parents. She'd have played that up, made it seem like there was major trouble in the family."

"You've got something behind that pretty face, Alsace."

"Most pretty girls do. Ode may be a bit flighty but I'd count on her having a few layers of guile under that. Brienda too, for that matter."

Morris smiles slightly to himself. "You know what the first cops on scene thought was wrong with Brienda? Wandering womb."

"Men." Alsace rolls her eyes. "Just because *your* anatomy controls your brain..."

"My brain is very much under its own control, thank you very much. Want to hop up there and see if there's a way to get the window open without unlocking it?"

"Not really." She eyes the uneven ornamentation that served as Brienda's ladder. "That'll hold you as easily as me."

"Yeah, but who'd catch me if I fall?"

"No one." Twyle's appearance from around the corner of the house actually startles a twitch from Morris. "It's mud and grass, nice soft landing. We need something to laugh at."

"Ha, ha."

"That wasn't a joke, Morris. Get up there and test the window."

After a shocked glance at the boss's face - which Twyle meets with his own steady, absolutely serious eyes - Morris sighs and applies himself to a more thorough study of the side of the house.

"I assume you brought Sedwin with you?" Alsace asks, turning towards Twyle to hide her smirk from Morris.

"He's in the house asking for one of Brienda's hairs."

"This isn't going to be like that metal-reading spell, is it? The office still smells like burnt copper."

"I found a spell that's supposed to get rid of that," Sedwin says, hurrying over to join them.

"Test it on your own time before you try it in my workplace," Twyle says. "And this had better not be like that. It's not like you've never done a tracking spell before, right?"

"Of course." Holding the pale gold hair carefully in one hand, Sedwin uscs the other to rummage through his pockets. "Copper chain...brown thread...eye of...damn..." Dropping the chain and thread into the hand with the hair, he spends a few minutes extricating a leaking jar from his pants pocket. He holds it up to the light and examines it. "Oh, good, most of them stayed in the bottle. Eye of newt..."

Alsace looks at the damp spot on the side of Sedwin's pants and takes a step back from him. "Please tell me you're not carrying around actual frogs or something in there."

"No, no, just pickled frogs' legs...okay." The wizard twists the hair and thread together and winds it around the chain. He has to put the jar of eyes down on the grass to get it open one-handed, and he pulls one out and leaves the jar there, open. Alsace takes a few steps further away. "Here goes..." He slides the chain through his fingers until he finds a socket that might have been meant for a jewel, and presses the newt eye into it. Holding the chain by one end, he starts spinning it slowly, muttering under his breath, pacing back and forth around the grass.

By the time Morris reaches the window, Sedwin is starting to look frustrated, his muttering growing in volume. The big detective glances down from his precarious perch. "Everything okay down there?"

"Just focus on the window, Morris," Twyle says - but he gives Sedwin a concerned look of his own.

The chain, which until now has showed no signs of movement on its own - no pointing the direction Brienda had gone, which it should have done - starts spinning faster than Sedwin's hand can keep up with. He lets go just before it bursts in midair, splattering him and Twyle both with bits of liquefied copper and pickled newt. Alsace is just outside the splash zone.

Sedwin falls over backwards. Twyle looks at him, one eyebrow raised.

"Not my fault, sir," the wizard protests, taking in the globs of metal, already solid again and starting to frost over, on Twyle's crisp lapels. "That was magic."

"It was supposed to be, at any rate," Twyle observes.

"No, no, I mean I hit something magic. The tracking spell got blocked."

"Really." Twyle looks around the side yard, as if something in the grass will tell him what had happened here.

"Explains the window, too," Morris calls down. "This is locked tight, no way in from outside. Either it was locked from inside after she left, or...magic."

"Magic." Twyle sighs. "Perfect."

Chapter 6

"ODE! THE POLICE ARE here again."

Mrs. Cadalan turns away from the stairs and glances nervously at the parlor door. Twyle has to smile at that; in most parts of town, no one would consider inviting the police into the parlor unless someone had died. For all the work people around here put into their pretty houses and perfect lawns, it's an illusion: a spirited attempt to draw a line between themselves and the people who don't have hedges - or hopefully erase the line between them and the people whose hedge-trimmers are held by servants. The servant-havers tend to put Twyle on a level with the butler and the garbage-men.

He makes the decision easier for her by showing himself into the kitchen.

"I checked on Ode five times in the night, just to make sure she was still there," Mrs. Cadalan says, following him and glancing back at the stairs. "I can't even imagine..."

"I wouldn't worry too much," Captain Twyle says. "One girl goes missing, that's cause for concern. Two best friends go missing at the same time, that's something they planned together. We would still do everything we can to find them and bring them home, of course - but we'd find them together and safe." Unless whoever took Brienda had been stalking both girls and wants the matched set, but telling a distraught mother that won't help anything.

Ode shuffles into the kitchen. She's dressed neatly enough, but she's pulled a bathrobe on over her blouse and skirt, and wears bed-slippers instead of shoes. Clearly she isn't planning on going anywhere today.

Mrs. Cadalan starts to make tea, but Twyle puts a hand on top of hers on the handle of the kettle. "I'd like to speak to your daughter alone, if that's alright."

She nods, nervously, then lets herself out the back door, taking something from the pile of gardening tools on her way out.

"Ode." The single syllable stops the girl as she's about to take a seat; she stays on her feet, turning to face Twyle. "Your friend was seen sneaking out her window the night she disappeared. From everything we've been told, if anyone would know where she was going, it's you." Ode stands, barely breathing, not quite meeting his eyes. "I know she had a fight with her parents that started at your house a few days ago. I know you know about it, and I know you lied about it. I need to know what else you lied about."

After a minute of staring down at the floor in thought, Ode unwraps one of her bracelets - though as it comes off it becomes clear why it looked like she was wearing so many; it's a long chain, more like a necklace, wrapped around several times. "He made her a few of these. It'll let you find anything she's got hidden in her room."

"He?"

"Her boyfriend. She was walking out with a - a student."

"A classmate?"

"No. A student wizard." Now Ode looks up at him, imploring. "You won't get him in trouble, will you? I know he's not allowed, but he was so sweet to her."

Twyle smiles, kindly. "A student, right? So he's not licensed yet? He's under no legal restrictions regarding his personal relationships yet, so I can't see how that's any of my business."

"It hardly makes sense anyway, telling wizards they can't fall in love and marry and - and...not that they were, you know..." The girl blushes.

"They weren't physically intimate, as far as you know?"

The polite phrasing fades her red cheeks slightly. "Not yet, but Brienda told me she thought it might happen soon."

"I'll need to know his name."

Ode shakes her head. "She never told me it. That was my idea, that she shouldn't tell anyone, even me, because it'll be easier to keep secret if no one knows enough to give it away, you know? Not that I'd tell on purpose, but I didn't want to know enough to really get him in trouble. But I think she's got a diary or something, it might say in there."

"I didn't find a diary in her room."

"You've got to use the charm. He gave her a bunch of them, there's one kind you wrap around a book or a piece of paper or whatever that makes it invisible, then another set that if you're touching it, you can see the stuff. She gave me one so we could pass notes in class."

"Ah, I see." Twyle winds the bracelet chain carefully and puts it in his breast pocket, next to his audiocast card. "Thank you for your help, Ode. If there's anything else you might need to tell us...?"

She shakes her head firmly. "That's it. That's the only thing I didn't tell you about before. Well, that and fighting with her parents, because I didn't want you looking too close at what she might be doing wrong."

"Just protecting your friend. Well, that's my job, too. Remember that."

Chapter 7

TWYLE HAS TO LAUGH when he finds Brienda's diary. With the charm her friend gave him in his hand, it's sitting there plain as day, right next to the pens on the nightstand. It's a simple paper-bound notebook, with another spell chain dropped casually on top of it - not all metal, he notices; there are a few paper-and-glue beads on it. He lifts it off the book and hands it to Sedwin.

"Of course," the wizard comments, more to himself than to Twyle. "He limited it so it only makes paper invisible. When it's touching paper, the charm and the paper both disappear."

"Of course," Twyle echoes drily. If it made sense it wouldn't be magic, right? "Look at the window, would you? See if you can figure out how she closed and locked it after her."

"Yes, sir."

With Sedwin keeping up a steady stream of muttering under his breath - mostly musing out loud, but Twyle hears the occasional incantation, too - the police captain sits down on the bed and opens the diary.

He's completely comfortable with invading her privacy; it's been his job for decades, dragging people's secrets into the light. It's because he knows exactly how easy it is to snoop through someone's things that he doesn't keep a diary himself, however useful it would be for sorting through his thoughts. Brienda, though, looks to be the sort of girl who trusts all her thoughts and dreams to paper, trusting the charm chain to keep anyone from reading it.

She'd written about her hopes of finding a way to marry her boyfriend without sacrificing his education and career. She'd written the details of more than a few vivid daydreams, which Twyle reads on the slim chance that they have any relevant information (they don't). And - yes! - she'd written his name. Kordell Manton.

According to Brienda, he's in his final year of studies at the Galedonia Institute of Magic. And she's so obviously smitten with him that if he'd asked her to run away with him, she would have.

Which doesn't change the situation much. If she'd married him, legally and properly, she'd have come back and told her parents. So either they're looking for a teen runaway and an un-celibate soon-to-be-licensed wizard - both illegal - or they're still investigating an abduction. Best not to even consider dropping the case.

"Sedwin, from what you've seen of his work so far, is this guy likely to be dangerous to us?"

The wizard stops muttering and shakes his head. "He's not bad for a student, probably better than I was, but none of the stuff he's done is anything special. The locking spell on this window, that's basic. I could've done it in my second year. And anyone can do an invisibility charm, the only tricky part is keeping it from making everything around it disappear. I don't think we'll need backup going after him. At worst he'll run and, well, we'll be right there on campus, there's plenty of professors there that can do a tracking spell better than I can even if I'm not good enough. We'd just have to ask, they'd do it right away if..."

"If we told them he had a girlfriend and was wanted for questioning in her disappearance."

"Yeah, well, they wouldn't care she'd disappeared. Sorry, sir, that's just how they are. But tell them he's seeing someone and they'll drag him back in for us."

Diary in his pocket, Twyle collects the rest of the team from downstairs on his way out of the house. The team has a vehicle - a brand new hovering cart, no horses needed, spelled to go as fast as twenty miles an hour if traffic allows - but it's hardly been used and he had, in fact, protested being given it at all. What's the point, he'd said, of a detective skimming along the streets so fast he doesn't see what's right under his nose? Whenever practical, the team walks.

In this case it's no hardship; even given the circuitous route the streets take, starting out towards downtown Dreeve and angling back towards the river in a wide u-bend curve to avoid the Mire, it's only an hour from the Woolsyth home to the GIM campus.

After some conversation Sedwin takes the lead once they reach the ivy-crusted brick buildings laid out around the green quad. Leaving the other three outside, he heads straight for the administrative offices - or as straight as the mazelike setup of the buildings allows.

"Good to see you, Sedwin." Sedwin has never learned the name of the cheerful middle-aged woman who works in the front office, but she seems to know every student by name. He eyes the jar of sweets on her desk, wondering if he can still get away with taking one. She has a box of tissues next to it, too, always full - this is the first stop for any student who has to change or drop a class mid-semester, a situation that often involves tears. "How's the real world treating you? I heard you were making charms for the police these days."

"Oh, not for all the police, just one team. I help with the investigations, too." He smiles, a bit proudly. "I mean, I'm not exactly a detective, but...it's good work."

She sees where his eyes are tracking and chuckles softly. "Help yourself. What can I do for you?"

He takes a sweet - just one, though - and holds off putting it into his mouth until after he's finished talking. "I'm looking for a student. Kind of a...a friend of a friend. Nothing really official, you know? I just could use to find him and...catch up. That sort of thing. His name's Kordell Manton."

"Kordell, yeah, I know him." As he starts sucking on the candy she rolls her chair back from the desk and opens a file drawer. "Good kid. A lot like you, really. Pushes himself too hard. He'd have an easier time of it with his classes if he'd relax every once in a while." It takes her less than thirty seconds to find the folder she's looking for, open it, and copy over some information to a fresh sheet of paper. "He's in History of Runic Magic now, you can probably catch him when it lets out in twenty minutes. There's his dorm number and class schedule on here."

"Thanks." He pauses awkwardly - it would have been easier if he'd known her name - and settles for a shy smile instead.

He snitches another candy before he leaves the office, and has finished off both of them by the time he finds the right building.

The classroom doesn't empty all at once; students wander out a few at a time, some stopping to talk to the professor first, or with classmates. Sedwin paces - not nervously, or at least no more nervously than any young wizard; too much stillness would stand out here. Every few minutes he glances at the description the office matron had written out.

The boy he's waiting for takes his time getting his notes packed up, but doesn't linger beyond that, and when he approaches the door he's more or less alone.

Sedwin wraps a hand around his upper arm and guides him even further from the clusters of chattering boys. "Walk with me."

"Who - "

"Police. We're looking for your girlfriend."

The look of faint concern that seems to be Manton's default expression shifts closer to panic. He glances around, but doesn't try to resist the firm hand that's steering him across the academic quad towards Sedwin's teammates, who are loitering under an oak tree trying not to draw attention.

"We need to talk to you," Sedwin says, "but I personally have no reason to give away your secrets, you understand me? Just keep walking and we'll get you back to our office quietly, no need for me to ask the whole school to help me find you. No need for me to tell them why I'm looking. Got it?"

The boy nods, and forces his face back towards his usual expression. It doesn't look natural or relaxed, he's pushed new lines into his forehead, but it won't alarm anyone at a casual glance.

"I don't know where she is."

"Don't tell me here, tell me at the office. You don't want to do this here, remember?"

Another nod, followed by a nervous swallow.

Chapter 8

THE TWO WIZARDS ARE chatting like old friends by the time they get to the towering police building in the heart of the city, complaining about professors they'd both had and swapping stories of student pranks. Somehow they even keep up a steady stream of conversation on the stairs, which are enough to leave all but the fittest police officers short of breath. Sedwin fumbles the door of the interview room, but the Manton boy barely seems to notice.

Twyle starts to follow them, but Morris puts a hand on his arm to stop him. "What's your approach, boss?"

"I'll keep it simple." Twyle looks down at Morris's hand, one eyebrow raised. The pressure the detective is holding him with increases slightly. "He's already nervous, I'll ask him questions until he answers them."

"Might tell you what he knows, but won't tell you what he is." As Twyle steps back from the door slightly, Morris lets go of him. "I'm not saying shake him up, but we need to get a feel for him. We don't want to ask him what he did to his girlfriend, we want to figure out what kind of guy he is, what kind of things he might be capable of."

"Not a bad thought," Twyle concedes. "You have a plan?"

"Send Alsace in first." Morris smiles slightly, that slow, secretive half-smile that usually means he's already three steps ahead of everyone else and enjoying every second of it. The Captain's eyes widen slightly, understanding dawning.

"And second?"

"Me."

Twyle thinks about it, but not for long. "Do it," he says. "Pull Sedwin out of there, I don't want them bonding right now. I'll find Alsace, tell her what we want."

"She probably knows better than you already."

It takes Twyle longer than usual to find Veryn Alsace, because she's been in the ladies' powder room on the next floor down. He spots her on her way back and gives her a questioning look. "You usually just use the gents' up here like the rest of us."

"Doesn't have a good enough mirror. You want me to talk to the boyfriend now, or is Morris going first?"

Twyle gives her an appraising look. She's fixed up her hair - tidy enough to begin with, but she's brushed it back to the chestnut shine it usually loses throughout the day. She still wears pants, same as usual, but she's put on a longer jacket that covers her hips, adding just a hint of feminine modesty - contradicted completely by the unlaced drape of her shirt collar.

He isn't an expert, but it looks like she's touched up her makeup, too.

"You," he says. She's clearly with the plan already and doesn't need him to explain it. "I'll have Morris join or replace you when the moment seems right."

She walks past Morris and Sedwin, straight into the interview room. Manton is sitting in one of the not-very-comfortable chairs around the small table; she smiles, and offers him her hand. "You're Kordell Manton, right? Veryn Alsace." When he reaches for her hand to shake it she leans forwards, reaching across the table to him, apparently not noticing how low the neckline of her blouse swings when she does that.

He looks. Not that that means much; most women look, never mind men. And it's only for a second.

"Have you heard anything about Brienda?" he asks.

Alsace shakes her head slightly. "She's your girlfriend, right?"

"Right. She...yes." His eyes unfocus slightly, his face closed off enough that only the habitual worry lines show.

"It must be tough, her being missing like this and you not being able to talk to anyone about it. Is there anyone you can talk to? Anyone who knows?"

The student wizard shakes his head. "I couldn't...I'd be expelled for sure, if anyone knew."

"That's such a pity, isn't it." She smiles, and leans in just enough to make it clear she's letting him in on a secret. "Wizards tend to be so handsome, it's really a shame you're all off limits."

The corners of his lips turn up slightly, but if he has any other reaction, he doesn't let it show.

"Is magic really worth it? Never being allowed to touch a girl?"

He shrugs, slightly. "I used to think so, before I met Brienda."

"Tell me about her."

"She wants to work with animals," he says, eyes still looking off into the distance somewhere. "Maybe go to veterinary school, if they'll let her in. They don't take many women. Her whole face lights up when she talks about it, though, like the whole future is just there and it all makes sense to her."

"How did you meet her?"

"At her school. One of my professors took me there, to talk to the boys about applying to GIM. I had lunch there, and she was at my table, and she...she made me laugh, you know? The way she tells jokes, it's just, you have to laugh."

Alsace's eyes haven't left his face the entire time they've been talking. She lets the smile fade slightly, though. "I wish I could find someone like that."

"I never thought I would." He either ignores or fails to notice the obvious invitation to comfort her. "But when I'm with her it's like, everything's okay, and nothing else matters." Finally, he meets Alsace's eyes. "Please tell me she's alright."

"She can't tell you that," Morris says, from the doorway behind Alsace. "She doesn't know. Boss wants you outside, dolly."

On her way out, safely out of Manton's sight, Alsace gives her fellow detective a glare that says he'll pay for that last word later, however useful it is in bringing out the suspect's feelings about women. She joins Twyle and Sedwin in the next room to listen to the rest of the interview.

"Anything useful?" Twyle asks. Alsace shakes her head.

"He likes women, I'm pretty sure about that, but he's not looking for fresh meat. I gave him plenty of chances. He turned it all back to Brienda. I don't know if it's true love forever, but he sure seems to feel like it is."

"Which doesn't mean he didn't do anything to her," Twyle concludes. "Plenty of people hurt people they love. Especially if she said something he didn't want to hear - a man who's just had his heart broken can be capable of anything."

"True," Alsace says, "but I'm not seeing any indication that he's a practiced hunter."

Twyle nods thoughtfully. "You and Morris seem to have this well in hand...I'll take Sedwin to search the boy's dorm room." He taps the breast pocket where he keeps his audiocast. "Call me if anything interesting comes up."

Chapter 9

"WE'LL NEED SOMEONE to let us in, sir," Sedwin points out, hesitating at a fork in one of the many footpaths that wind around the Galedonia Institute of Magic campus. Left to the administrative buildings, or right towards the student housing building where Manton lives? "They keep all the dorms locked."

Twyle shakes his head and takes the right fork towards the dorms. He glances at the names carved in ornamental stonework over the building doors, and when he finds the one they're looking for, he bypasses the front door and circles the building. Near the less-decorated side entrance he glances around - there's no one in sight - and casually lifts one of the bricks that line the edge of the path. Something has scratched the bottom repeatedly, leaving a key-shaped mark. And in the paler square of dirt the brick revealed, pressed into a permanent-looking indentation, is the key. "Some things never change." He unlocks the side door, then puts the key and brick back where they were.

"Sir?"

"I used to be young, Sedwin."

"I didn't know you'd studied here, though."

Twyle glances at Sedwin, or perhaps through him, eyes slightly unfocused. "I didn't."

Sedwin opens his mouth again, but something in Twyle's expression stops him from asking.

Manton has left the door to his room unlocked. Not entirely uncommon; theft of thesis topics is probably more frequent here than theft of belongings.

"If our boy's got any dark secrets, he's not too paranoid about guarding them." Twyle nudges the door open and takes a good look around before he steps inside.

At first glance Kordell Manton seems like a good match for Brienda in terms of tidiness; he's left his laundry on the floor. "They'd better hire a maid if they ever live together."

"And maybe a cook." Sedwin lifts a green bowl off the desk, where it had been serving as a paperweight. The contents had probably been soup before it dried out. The wizard makes a face and puts it back down. "Anything in particular we're looking for?"

"Well, if you see a paper that says "Note to self: girlfriend's body is buried under the oak tree by the Applied Charms building," let me know. Otherwise, just keep your eyes open."

"He's taking Structural Technomancy," Sedwin says, paging through the papers on the desk. "Tough class. Looks like he might be passing it, too." There's an uncharacteristic edge to his voice - awe or jealousy, maybe.

"Keep your eyes open *quietly*, Sedwin."

Twyle wraps the anti-invisibility charm around his hand in case it will reveal anything hidden here, but it doesn't - either because it isn't keyed right or because Manton isn't hiding anything. The boy had taken copious stacks of notes on his classes, and has obviously been reading through and studying from them, but if Brienda has sent him any love letters, he's either gotten rid of them or hidden them very well.

No sketches, no half-written poems. No indication of which pile of underwear on the floor is clean and which is dirty. There are three mugs scattered at random around the desk: one holding cold tea, one empty apart from a brown-stained ring halfway up, one damp inside and slightly fuzzy.

"You think they'll stay together? If he didn't do it, I mean...and, I mean, if we find her."

Twyle doesn't answer. He starts methodically disassembling the bed, pulling back the sheets one at a time.

"I wonder if she's ever seen this place." Sedwin keeps musing out loud, seeming entranced by a few margin notes in a Metal Charms textbook. "Probably not, I mean, a girl would really stand out in here. I mean, her room's messy, but not like..." He leans over the third mug, jerks an arm up over his mouth, and sneezes. "I wonder if she knows how he lives. If I was thinking of moving in with a housemate who lives like this...well...I wouldn't."

"Check under the top drawer," Twyle says. "That style of desk, it's usually roomy underneath. Good place to hide things."

"Yes, sir." Sedwin pulls the top drawer out and turns it over, dumping the contents onto the desk chair. "Nothing stuck to the bottom, nothing in the desk under it."

Twyle sighs and, charm still in his hand, reaches over and lifts the chain off the envelope taped to the underside of the drawer. "Look again."

"Oh...right. I should have realized."

Twyle opens the envelope and here, finally, is some evidence that the man who lives in this room is fond of girls. Half a dozen letters in the same hand as Brienda's journal (she'd done a neater job on the letters, though; she tended to scribble and scratch things out in her diary). Three pencil-and-paper drawings, done by someone who isn't a very good artist but was clearly fascinated by certain aspects of the subject, gleaming hair and a curved chest sketched large out of proportion to the rest of the girl. Twyle rolls his eyes. Manton got the face completely wrong and, really, the bust too. No one would know it was supposed to be Brienda if he hadn't written her name under each picture.

There's no reference to where she might be now.

"You think Morris will get anything from him?" Sedwin asks, leaning over Twyle's shoulder.

"No." Twyle stuffs everything back in the envelope and puts it in his pocket alongside the diary. "I think Alsace will."

"Loser buys dinner for the team?"

That startles a smile out of the Captain. "Sure, what the hell."

Chapter 10

"SO WHERE'VE YOU GOT Brienda stashed, anyway?"

Morris has his chair pushed back, feet up on the table between him and Kordell Manton. The wizard hasn't gotten any less twitchy, and the detective isn't even trying to help.

"I don't know," Manton protests. "It wasn't me, I didn't - I don't know where she is."

"Look, I won't really care if you did." Morris folds his arms and grins. "Just give me a turn with her, you know? I know how to cover that sort of thing up."

The boy just shakes his head and stares.

"Some of your classmates, they really know how to have a good time, you know what I'm saying? You ever been to those parties they have over at Stannow Hall? No, you wouldn't have, you only like girls." Morris laughs. "Well, at least you've got Brienda. Oh, right, of course you don't, but I'm sure you had her already, right? Pretty girl, I've seen pictures. Wouldn't even have to turn her over. Girls like face to face, especially when they're that...sweet."

Manton's face, which started out almost unnaturally pale, is steadily darkening until his scraggly bits of beard actually blend in. "It wasn't like that with, we never, she didn't..."

"Ah." Morris's smile changes, the corners less pointed, not as much of a glint in the eye - sympathetic rather than laughing at the world. "Afraid you won't impress her? Don't worry, everyone's nervous at first. All you need is some practice. My friend Veryn - you remember Veryn, she was in here talking to you earlier? Talk about wild. She could show you a thing or two. Might even give you a pity discount because of your girlfriend being missing. How about it?"

"No." The boy shakes his head, eyes so wide it almost looks like he might dislodge them. "That's not...no."

"Really, kid, don't worry about...it." Morris's glance, seeming to pierce through the solid table and Manton's trousers, leaves nothing unspecified. "From all I've heard Brienda's a virgin, and trust me, bigger is not always better. Whatever you've got will do fine."

Since disappearing into the floor isn't an option, Manton settles for trying to make himself smaller, pulling his legs up, arms in, and head down. He shakes his head again, but doesn't try to say anything.

"You about ready for a break, Morris?"

Manton reacts to Veryn Alsace's appearance in the doorway with equal parts relief and further embarrassment; he lifts his head to look at her, but his limbs seem to shrink back even further.

"I don't know, we're just getting to know each other here."

"That wasn't actually a question."

Morris takes his time leaving, looking long and deep into Manton's eyes first. As he walks past Alsace he puts a hand on her shoulder and leans in. "I don't know what he is," he says, "but I know what he's not."

The wizard stares at the door for a few minutes after it closes, carefully avoiding looking at her.

"Is something wrong?" Alsace puts her notebook on the table, straightens the chair, and sits.

"He, uh...he was trying to whore you out."

"What, again?" She rolls her eyes. "Ignore him. We all do. Now, where did we leave off earlier? I think you were telling me how you and Brienda met."

"I, uh...maybe?"

Alsace frowns, turns a few pages in her notebook, makes a notation. "Let's skip ahead, though. Start at the end and work backwards. Can you tell me about the last time you saw her?"

"It was...that night." He chokes a little on the words. "You know, the night she didn't come home?"

"Mhm." The detective bites the end of her pen, staring down at her notes. "How was she?"

"She was...fine, you know? Like normal. It was all just like normal."

"Remind me what normal is? What's your routine when you meet her?"

"We wait until it's late enough that no one will notice - usually an hour, hour and a half before midnight - and meet by the river. That night was like all the other times, we talked for a while, then I went back to my dorm and she went...you know, home."

"Walk me through it, minute by minute. Everything she said, every expression on her face, what she was wearing, what you did - everything." She turns to a blank page in her notebook.

Chapter 11

EVEN NOW, IN THE MIDDLE of the day, the footpath along the river isn't particularly bustling. It takes a particular mindset, and possibly a blindfold, to enjoy a pleasant stroll along the most polluted stretch of water. It isn't as bad as it used to be - a decade or two earlier the entire river ran a dizzying foam of garish colors - but the curve around the Institute of Magic and the other magic-related businesses that have sprung up near it is still a technicolored mess. Even Sedwin and Manton are trying not to look too closely at the water.

"Here," Manton says, putting his hand against a tree-trunk - one of the few old enough to have set deep roots before the river started poisoning the plants along its banks. "This w - this is our spot. I tried doing a tracking spell from here because, you know, it's the last place I saw her, but...I guess I did a really good job on that anti-tracking spell I did on her."

Sedwin touches the tree, fingers finding a lump of green-tinged copper that doesn't quite match the moss and bark. "Isn't magic fun," he mutters. Twyle glances at the metal splatters and self-consciously adjusts his jacket collar - his second-best suit jacket, not that a casual observer would find it any less crisp and tailored than the one he'd left in the care of his cleaning service.

"So you met her here that night," Twyle says, paging through his notes for the look of it though he remembers every word the missing girl's boyfriend had said in his interviews. "And you had - skipping over some details which I'm sure are irrelevant - a perfectly normal lovers' conversation. And then?"

"Then, well, we had to get home. I headed back across the river - the bridge is right there - " He points to a stone footbridge across the narrowest point in the river. "I went back to my room and got a couple hours of sleep before I had to get up for class."

"And she went back to her house?" Twyle asks. He waves an arm towards the road, which follows the river for a while before turning south and circling back around to Brienda's neighborhood. "That way?"

"No, she didn't like taking the long way around because she thought her parents would notice if she stayed out too long. She went - she always went that way. Straight line back to her house."

All four members of the team turn to look where Manton is pointing, into the network of alleys and dirt paths - mud paths, really - that lead due south from the river. None of them say anything, but then, none of them need to make the obvious comments about the risks of a girl as young and naive as Brienda walking alone, in the dark after-midnight hours, through a place like the Mire.

Manton is a little slower to understand, but he can read their expressions, even if he can't read the streets. "I should have walked her home, shouldn't I," he says. "Or at least made sure she stayed on the main streets."

"That would have been the smart thing to do, yes," Twyle says. "Morris, what does this do to your theory that she was taken by someone she knew?"

"Tears it right to shreds." For a rarity, the man looks slightly puzzled. "I thought even a stranger would know what kind of home situation they were grabbing her from and wouldn't want to risk it, but if she was out there alone...it could have been anything."

"So we start over. New crime scene, new search for evidence, new theories. Manton, we're done with you for now, just try not to do anything stupid." The boy nods gratefully, and heads for the footbridge.

Twyle watches him go, then turns back to his team. "Let's walk her path home, see what we can learn."

The main street is paved with broad cobblestones; the side road Brienda took is dirt - at first. The city had graded the paving high enough to keep the heavily-trafficked main street dry despite being so close to the river. In the process, though, they'd blocked the natural drainage of the area beyond, putting land that had been well hydrated to begin with in a state of perpetual sog. Sedwin balks at the first mud-puddle.

"Please," Alsace scoffs, letting her sturdy ankle-high boots take the brunt of it. "You have no problem with animal parts dripping down your pants pocket but you draw the line at this?"

The wizard skirts the edge of the first puddle, but half a block further on it becomes clear that avoiding the mud entirely isn't an option. Sedwin mutters under his breath and tries to pick his steps carefully; Twyle and Morris plow forwards, keeping their heads up as if not looking at their feet will make something better. Only Alsace seems unconcerned. "Could be worse," she comments, after the third time Sedwin pauses to try to figure out what his shoe has splashed in. "Could be cow shit. Some things I do not miss."

"No, the cattle pens were west of here. Close, though," Twyle says.

"Seriously?" Alsace laughs. "I meant my father's farm, but...there were actually cows in the city?"

"When I was growing up." The Captain smiles wryly. "Not that long ago, really. We import everything now, the wizards make frozen barges for meat, it gets shipped in from outside the city...used to be we had to slaughter it fresh. This is all new since then." He waves a hand at the shoddy warehouses, all of them elevated enough to keep the floors dry...more or less. Most of the stairs and some of the more derelict buildings' window-openings are occupied, though hardly anyone is looking directly at the four cops. "Trying to keep up with the economy shifting, find new local industries to fill in the gaps left by all the stuff we buy from other places now..."

As they pass, three people lounging on a bare, splintering wood stoop - hardly more than a stair-frame at this point - exchange a few whispers and slip sideways into the shadows between buildings.

Most of his attention on Twyle's speech, Sedwin drags a foot through another puddle, barely seeming to notice. "Should we be asking people if they've seen Brienda?"

Twyle glances around, then shakes his head. "Not yet, no."

"Really? I mean, if she disappeared around here..."

"Disappeared?" A pile of rags on the side of the road springs upright and latches onto Sedwin's arm. "Disappeared from here, and you're even looking? Hah. What's being done to find my boy?"

Twyle gently extracts Sedwin's hand from the woman's grip, putting his own hand in hers instead. "What's your name?"

She gives him a blank-eyed stare before answering. "Minnie, sir, Minnie Kyne."

Twyle steers her over to the steps of a building, where they can both sit, and takes out his notebook. As soon as the notebook leaves his pocket she starts to pull away from him. He puts it back, smiles patiently, and motions her to sit. "I'd like to look for your son," he says. "That will be easier if you tell me about him and let me take notes."

She shuffles slowly over to the steps and sits next to him. "My boy is Essery, he's ten years old and been gone a week."

"Do you have a place where you usually stay, or any family in the area?" Twyle asks, getting the notebook out again.

She shakes her head. "Just here, wherever we can find out of the wind. And I've got no family. No husband, either, I know that's what you're wondering." Twyle shakes his head slightly, as if to indicate the thought hadn't crossed his mind. "He said he'd marry me, but when I told him there was a baby coming and it'd better be now, he told me oh, no, he had a wife already, he's so sorry he's done this to me...ten years gone and not a word from him since but, oh, he did say he was *sorry*..."

"Sounds like he was a bit late to think through the right and wrong, miss. Could you tell me when and where you last saw Essery, and what he looks like?"

"He's big for ten," she says, a little proudly. "I feed him all I can, it's not always enough but he's been growing nicely."

Twyle finds a blank page, then looks at the rest of the team. "Spread out and start talking to people. Especially the ones who seem like they don't want to talk. Don't bother asking if they saw anything, just ask if they know anyone who's gone missing around here. Veryn - " Alsace glares at the Captain, clearly daring him to tell her to be careful or stay with one of the men. He sighs, and his gaze shifts to Sedwin for a moment. "Look, just - everyone stay within sight of the team, alright? We should all keep an eye out for each other."

"Don't worry, Captain." Morris pats Twyle on the shoulder. "I'll watch your back."

Chapter 12

BACK AT THE POLICE headquarters downtown, the team paces eagerly in their shared office. Though the inner room - Twyle's private office - is arranged just the way he wants it, the outer office is a bit less functional; the three desks look well used and set up to their occupants' preferences, but the walls and floor space look like no one's quite finished unpacking and moving in yet.

"We know about Brienda and the Kyne boy, in addition to which I heard about another disappearance, a woman in her twenties, during the night about a week ago. There was an actual witness to that one who saw her being put in a cart by a group of men." Twyle starts moving the boxes that are stored in front of the map of the city pinned on one of the office walls. "Did you get anything?"

"It was, you know, hard to make sense of what the man was saying, I think he wasn't...quite all there," Sedwin says, "but I think his friend disappeared. Another man. Might've been last night or ten years ago, he wasn't very clear on that."

Twyle nods. "Morris?"

"Four." He doesn't elaborate, but does stick four pins in the map. "What did you get, Alsace?"

"Three drunken marriage proposals, one of which I might consider if he takes a bath. And eight stories of people gone missing."

"Eight?" Twyle raises an eyebrow.

"People seemed quite eager to talk to me."

Twyle takes four pins, hands one to Sedwin, and passes the rest of the box to Alsace. "Were any of them witnessed?"

"One," Morris says. "Night, men, cart. Same as yours."

"Three of mine just noticed someone wasn't there anymore, but the other five saw or heard something. Screaming, mostly, from the person being grabbed. They weren't very quiet about it. One of my suitors got a good look and said there were three men. He described them as big, and this coming from a man who must be over six feet tall if he stands up straight."

"Discounting Sedwin's man, what are the oldest and most recent dates of disappearances?"

"Three weeks ago, and last night," Morris says.

"I had one at three and a half weeks," Alsace adds.

"So let's say over the last month. Sixteen that we know about, so there have to be more. Ages and genders?"

Morris is quickest to answer. "Three boys, one girl. All between twelve and twenty."

"Male," Sedwin says, with a shrug. "Who knows about the age. Might've even been the same person as one of the ones you heard about."

"About an even split of men and women," Alsace says. "I'm not entirely clear on all the ages but certainly no children, no elderly people."

Twyle takes in the pins in the map. "Morris, I would appreciate your thoughts. If we assume all these disappearances are related, that they were done by the same person or group of people - why were they taken, and what sort of criminal are we looking for?"

"Not for one person's personal pleasures, certainly. Not that many and that varied." Morris leans back against the edge of his desk, making himself comfortable. "The Kyne boy - he's our youngest, ten, but his mother said he's big for his age. I'd say they're not stocking a brothel, either, or they'd take younger and smaller." Sedwin looks shocked, but Twyle and Alsace just nod thoughtfully. "The people they're targeting, they all look strong and able to work." He chuckles. "Whoever took them might even be telling themselves they're doing these homeless people a favor by putting them to work and getting them under a roof before winter comes."

"Say that's true, and we're looking for a workhouse," Twyle says. "How far would they be willing to transport people? They were all taken within the Mire."

"Not far. They'd be afraid of getting caught, and probably too lazy to go too far. There's homeless people all over the city, after all. We'll find them in the same neighborhood they were taken from."

Chapter 13

THE SWISH OF SANDPAPER is quiet enough that conversation would have been easy enough, except the smell of varnish discourages the idea of drawing that much breath. A few of the workmen look nervously at the four detectives, but none of them stop working. It's difficult to tell how the piles of surfaces and posts will turn into tables, but, well, that's no concern of the police.

The men all look clean, willing if not enthusiastic about their work, and seem to have all their fingers - not always a given in industrial woodworking. Twyle finishes his circuit of the floor and shakes the foreman's hand. "Thank you for your cooperation."

The mud outside the building hasn't improved since the day before, but at least it's cold enough to keep the smell of rot down, or perhaps the team has acclimated to the smell after a long day of searching the Mire. Even Twyle draws a few relieved breaths of varnish-fume-free air as he steps out the door and walks down the street to the next building.

He knocks on the door, and stands patiently for several minutes before it's opened.

"Mind if we come in and look around?" Twyle holds his badge up for inspection. "We're looking for a runaway girl who might be hiding around here."

"I, I, uh...I don't think I can let you in." The door stays open a precise six inches, the bespectacled manager's body blocking it from opening further. "Maybe come back when the boss is here?"

"Of course." Twyle smiles politely as the door is pushed shut in his face.

"On to the next?" Sedwin asks. Twyle doesn't even bother to nod.

"Last one on the block," Alsace observes. "How many more streets after this?"

Twyle checks his list. "Last one."

"Let's get it over with, then."

The warehouse isn't exactly quiet and empty as they approach, but the walls are tilted more than most, windows broken, the front door hanging open slightly. "Oh, good, another derelict," Morris says. "First one to put a foot through the floor writes all our reports for us."

"Morris."

He glances at Twyle. "Kidding, boss." He pushes the door back and forth a few times, listening to the hinges creak. "Do we announce ourselves and shout for permission if anyone's home, or just go in?"

Despite the dim light, the interior is obviously empty, apart from faint scurrying sounds - rats, mostly, maybe a few homeless people already showing themselves out the back door. "Just go in," Twyle says.

The space had been divided into rooms at some point, but the interior walls have crumbled even further than the outer. Twyle pokes at a few piles of blankets that could have been big enough to hide a person, but leaves everything where it is. No one's hiding one person here, let alone a dozen or more. He looks up - the ceiling has a few gaping holes in it, giving a glimpse of the second floor and, beyond it, the rafters. "Sedwin," he says. "You're the lightest. Go to the top of the stairs - stand in place, don't walk around up there - and shine a light around, see if there's anything up there."

The wizard eyes the rickety staircase with apprehension, but hurries up it without protest. He's back in a matter of minutes. "Nothing but more rats."

"Back to the office?" Morris asks. Twyle shakes his head, and lets the rest of the team follow him back to the main streets and around to a bluff overlooking the swamp.

It has a surprisingly good view of most of the mud paths and warehouses. Twyle looks at his watch. "Two minutes to six."

"Ah." Morris nods in understanding and sweeps his eyes over the lowlands.

It's less than two minutes before the first bell starts ringing - there's always a bit of uncertainty; not all of them take their time from regulated clocks. It's obvious when the factory clocks turn six, though, because the doors open and a weary crowd flows out onto the streets.

Even at a tired walking pace, it doesn't take long for the crowds to thin and the district to settle down for the evening. "What did you see?"

Sedwin glances around, waiting for someone else to go first. Alsace shrugs. "That second-to-last place that wouldn't let us in let out as many workers as any of them. Wasn't there one somewhere over there, though..." She waves a hand towards the left. "We were there early in the afternoon."

"There," Morris says, pointing more definitely. "Wouldn't let us in, said we'd disrupt production. I only saw two or three people leave."

Twyle nods and checks his list. "I've got the factory owner as a Mr. Caldwell Fraley. Makes parts for spells and technomagicks. Could be our place."

Sedwin shakes his head. "Using coerced labor for magic supplies? That sort of thing matters, you'd get inferior goods out of it. Someone would notice."

"Notice and do what?" Twyle shakes his head. "Complain about audiocasts dropping calls and buses giving bumpy rides? Morris, settle in here and keep an eye on Fraley's place overnight. I'll get the paperwork started for search authorizations for everywhere we couldn't look today. Sedwin, Alsace...go home. It'll be a long day tomorrow."

Chapter 14

THE HILLTOP IS A LOT more busy the next morning. "No movement overnight that I could see," Morris says, deftly inserting himself right behind Twyle in the crowd of uniformed officers gathering around the Captain. "But it gets pretty dark down there. No streetlights, only a couple of the factories are lit."

"I'll make sure to complain to the City Council about that." Twyle doesn't turn around.

"Yeah, I'm sure they'll fix it as soon as they hear." Morris rolls his eyes. "Rest of the team here?"

"Any minute now." Twyle waves over another captain, this one - unlike him and his team - uniformed. Twyle's eyes linger on the copious amounts of gold braid on the man's otherwise simple brown coat, but he keeps his thoughts to himself. "Get your men organized. I want about twenty with me and my team, the rest split into seven groups to execute searches on these warehouses." He hands the man a list. "Fast but thorough, and remember, you're only looking for missing people. I don't want anyone throwing their weight around because they think someone's work permits aren't in order."

"We're hitting Fraley's?" Morris asks. Twyle nods.

"I've got a pretty good feeling. Simultaneous searches so if we're wrong, we don't give the other factories time to hide much...but four men apiece will do the job."

Some sort of joke hovers at the corners of Morris's mouth, but Sedwin's arrival interrupts it. The commotion of policemen being shouted into groups extends the pause in conversation; by the time Alsace shows up, it's clear which twenty are staying with the team.

"We really need this many just to search a factory?" she asks.

"Best case, no, but..." Twyle's lips tighten.

The mud of the roads isn't any better after being trampled and splashed by the mass of men ahead of them. It isn't at all a subtle approach; by the time they reach the first run-down building, there's no one in sight on the streets. A few flickers of motion mark the last few street people disappearing into the shadows.

Fraley's is one of the newer and sturdier buildings; the factory has only been open a couple months, and parts of it are actually built of stone and cement rather than the standard thin, bare boards.

Twyle's knock echoes through an unnaturally quiet street.

A nervous cough from inside gives away that someone's there, but it takes a few minutes for the window - not the door next to it - to open. "Same answer today as yesterday, Captain," the slightly rotund, red-faced man says - he has the sort of complexion that suggests just pushing the window open was a strenuous exercise. "Can't stop production to let you in, no matter how many men you bring with you."

The window starts to close, but Twyle stops it in one hand and shoves a rolled paper at the man. "I've got orders to search this building. Signed and legal. We're coming in with your cooperation or not. You've got three choices here: open the door, go get the owner so he can open the door, or get out of the way so you don't get hurt when we knock the door down."

"There's a fourth option in there too," Morris adds. He doesn't smile. "You don't have to get out of the way."

"I am the owner." If a grimace could be smug, this one is. "And that door is not going to be opened in any way. We make parts for magic equipment here, the presence of the wrong person in the workroom could completely destroy their usefulness."

"That's not my problem." Twyle takes a step sideways - closer to the window, practically in Fraley's face, and clearing space in front of the door. "You have thirty seconds to open that door before my men bring up the battering ram."

The window slams shut. Twyle counts slowly under his breath, but nothing else happens.

When he gets to thirty, he takes another step away from the door and beckons to four men in the middle of the brown-uniformed crowd. They take their time getting into position, lining up the battering ram at what they judge to be the perfect angle - but when it finally connects, it's enough to shake the building across the street.

The door doesn't budge.

"Again," Twyle orders.

The second swing has the same results as the first, give or take a few pieces of debris falling from neighboring buildings.

He lets them keep trying, but walks down the steps to have a quiet word with Sedwin while they do. When five minutes of steady hammering doesn't so much as wobble the door, Twyle calls them off. The wizard eyes the factory nervously.

"I - I don't know, sir..." His fingers twitch, maybe sketching something in the air. "I mean, it's not something I usually do on purpose, you know?"

"So do things by accident until it works." Twyle gives Sedwin a pat on the shoulder, then a gentle shove towards the stairs.

Sedwin mutters the whole way up, nods to himself a few times, then fishes a piece of chalk out of his jacket pocket and starts drawing on the door.

"Might be a good idea to stand back," Twyle comments to Alsace and Morris. The rest of the men take their lead and give the door a wide berth.

A QUESTION OF IMPORT

It takes about fifteen minutes of Sedwin poking at the door with his piece of chalk, but then there's a boom almost as loud as the battering ram was - and far more effective.

Chapter 15

THE FIRST THUD STARTLES the woman next to Brienda into dropping the sheet of tin she's holding. Brienda helps her pick it up and slide it into place on the worktable, but nearly drops it herself when there's another thud a few seconds later.

"Oy!" The foreman, on his elevated platform just inside the workroom door, shouts loudly enough that the room would have echoed from it even without magical amplification. "No one told any of you to stop working!"

Brienda adjusts the position of the tin sheet - she's been in trouble before for helping the workers next to her, and also for talking to them; she doesn't even know the name of the woman who's supposed to position the heavy sheets of tin, or the boy who's supposed to clear them off after Brienda has done her job. She helps anyway, because the metal pieces are so big the woman can barely manage them alone.

Given the smell of old gin on the woman's clothes, it doesn't take a genius to figure out why she shakes and drops things so often. Brienda has learned to fake a few shakes herself, because the overseers seem to think they've rescued her from some vile drug habit. Contradicting them doesn't seem like a good idea.

Tuning out the now-constant background thumping, she starts turning the handle on the tin press. The first few turns are easy but once it touches the tin, she has to push it hard enough to shape and cut the metal. She doesn't own a portable audiocast - her family had only last year gotten the big one in the hall - but she's seen enough of them to recognize the shape, squares a couple inches on a side with a textured pattern pressed into them.

She's gotten the metal cut through and the press lifted by the time the noise stops. The boy glances up at the door as if expecting something else to happen now, but Brienda nudges him under the table and he starts clearing the metal cards off and stacking them in his box.

"Another sheet," she whispers, shooting a warning look at the woman, whose blouse is already torn in a few places where the foreman's whip had cut through it.

The woman nods and starts fumbling another piece of metal into place.

Maybe that was it; maybe everything is back to normal now, no more loud noises and shaking floors. Brienda keeps her eyes on her work, turning the handle - again - and again - to cut a big square of metal into a lot of little squares of metal.

It isn't particularly interesting work. She gives it her full attention anyway.

Another sound - more boom than thud this time - makes her jump just as the press touches the tin. Hoping it hasn't distorted the pieces enough that anyone will notice, she keeps turning.

There are more sounds; shouts, footsteps - thuds, sounding smaller and closer than the first. Fight sounds.

"Someone's broken in," the woman whispers.

"Not our problem," the boy whispers back as Brienda gives the wheel its final turn and breaks through the tin. "Work until someone tells us to stop."

The foreman turns to look out the door - wondering, no doubt, whether he should join the fight, stay where he is, or run - but three men in police uniforms push their way in before he makes up his mind. He's grabbed and unceremoniously wrestled to the ground.

The fourth man into the room isn't uniformed, but he isn't one of the factory men, either; a middle-aged man - hair going salt-and-pepper just over the ears - wearing a crisp suit.

"We're looking for Brienda Woolsyth and Essery Kyne." The speaking platform amplifies the man's quiet words. "We'll also help anyone else who's here against their will."

"That's me," the boy says, hands shaking over the audiocast blanks he hasn't cleared off the workbench yet. "That's my name. How come the law're looking for me?"

"Me too. Don't worry," Brienda says. "I think they're looking for everyone, they just don't know all the names. Come on." She nudges the woman working on her other side towards the steps. "Let's get everyone into a line there. Nice and orderly. They're here to help us, I'm sure, they're here to get us out."

Neither the woman nor Essery look convinced, but the woman starts walking towards the stairs when Brienda gives her another gentle push. It doesn't take much to get the people at the next workbench moving, too - tired and used to following directions, they do what Brienda suggests without thinking about it.

She wraps an arm around Essery and helps him to the front of the line - he's shaking so much he seems likely to fall over any second. The crisp-suited policeman is coming down the stairs by the time they get there.

"I'm Brienda Woolsyth," she tells him, "and this is Essery. We're the ones you asked for. And I'd appreciate it if you'd give him something to eat, they've had him on half rations because he wasn't doing enough work."

Chapter 16

IN THE OLDER PART OF the police building, a section with so contrasting a personality it may as well have been a different building, an entire hallway has been set aside for the offices of the Law Enforcement Reform Oversight Commission - technically employees of the governor and not the police department, but they have to be where the police are to do their jobs. Captain Twyle walks to the last heavy oak door on the hall and nods politely to the chairman's secretary in the outer office.

"He's in," she says, returning the nod without looking up from her work.

"Thank you." Twyle shows himself into the inner office. "Chairman Louzain. You received my report, I hope?"

"Punctual as usual." Louzain taps a folder on his desk to indicate it. "Come in, sit down. Anything to add that didn't make it into the written version?"

"Not that I'm aware of, sir. I'll send an addendum if I learn of anything."

"Just what we need, more addenda." Louzain opens the report. "Bad enough you included written reports from the constables who first got the case."

"I wanted those there for contrast, sir. To show why I took the case away from them."

Louzain sighs. "I think I know the answer but let's do this by the book. Why did you choose this case? What made you feel that it wouldn't be adequately handled by the men assigned to it?"

"Because they'd given up before I even got there." Twyle grimaces, then takes a seat. "They assumed a teenage girl was so inherently untrustworthy that her disappearance wasn't worth investigating."

"I don't think anyone will contest you on this one, but rules are rules." Louzain pulls his ashtray closer and starts tapping his pipe out into it. "You're the governor's experiment here. A test of how police work could be done better. You picked your team, you pick your cases, we've given you more leeway than any other detective on the force and you answer to practically no one - but after you're done, the commission has to pick apart your every move, just to make sure you haven't let it go to your head."

"Yes, sir."

"You're good on this one, I think. You took a case no one else wanted and you did wonders with it." He takes his audiocast out of his pocket - careful to touch it only by the edges so it doesn't activate - and looks at it. "Any chance these damn things will be more reliable now?"

"I doubt it, sir. We shut down one source of sub-standard parts for them, but..."

"Who knows where else this stuff is coming from." The device drops back into the chairman's pocket. "Right, of course."

"Did you have anything else to discuss, sir?"

"I've got a note from bookkeeping about your expenses on this investigation..." The chairman coughs. "Quite a hefty bill from your tailor included there, I understand."

"Yes, it turned out a new jacket would cost the department quite a bit less than having the old one cleaned and repaired."

A raised eyebrow. "Damaged on the job, I take it?"

"Yes, sir."

There's a lengthy pause; the option of pushing the matter further clearly considered, then rejected.

"Leave it to you to close cases we didn't even know we had." Louzain frowns at his unlit pipe, then fumbles in his pocket for more tobacco. "Twenty-three missing persons recovered, I hear. One law for everyone, eh, Twyle? No case too small." The chairman chuckles appreciatively.

Twyle's face doesn't show much, but he doesn't answer, or laugh along with Louzain.

"Something on your mind, man?"

"One law, the same for everyone?" Twyle crosses his arms and leans back in the chair - Louzain has comfortable furniture, even for guests to his office. "Except it wasn't, sir, was it. I wasn't even looking for twenty-two of them. They got lucky that a girl from a better neighborhood got caught up in this."

"What else could you have done? We didn't even know they were missing."

"We should have." Twyle looks Louzain in the eye until the man begins to fidget uncomfortably. "For myself, for my own team...we couldn't have done anything better, sir. But we should have had people out there. There shouldn't be streets the police don't walk on and people the police don't listen to."

"There's only so much we can do about the lives these people choose for themselves." Louzain idly pages through the report. "And I see you did your best to make arrangements for the care of the victims."

"And notified their families where possible, sir." Twyle's lips tighten into something that's probably a smile, though it doesn't look happy. "With some success, but not perfectly. I wasn't able to reach Magistrate Hobart to notify him that his son Essery had been found safe, though his wife was able to take quite a detailed message for him."

Louzain stiffens slightly, then sighs. "Leaving another mess for us to deal with, I suppose."

"Not us, sir. The city has plenty of divorce attorneys who will be happy for the work."

Don't miss out!

Visit the website below and you can sign up to receive emails whenever Rachel Caren Kisala publishes a new book. There's no charge and no obligation.

https://books2read.com/r/B-A-YRDX-URDGC

BOOKS2READ

Connecting independent readers to independent writers.

About the Author

Rachel Caren Kisala is a spinster who's spent most of her life in Brighton, Massachusetts. She enjoys cooking, gardening, knitting, and the color purple.